NIGHT RIDE

By BERNIE & MATI KARLIN
Illustrated by BERNIE KARLIN

SIMON AND SCHUSTER
BOOKS FOR YOUNG READERS
Published by
Simon & Schuster Inc., New York

SIMON AND SCHUSTER
BOOKS FOR YOUNG READERS

Simon & Schuster Building,
Rockefeller Center,
1230 Avenue of the Americas,
New York, New York 10020.

SIMON AND SCHUSTER BOOKS FOR YOUNG READERS
is a trademark of Simon & Schuster Inc.

Designed by Bernie Karlin
Manufactured in the United States of America
10 9 8 7 6 5 4 3 2 1
Library of Congress Cataloging-in-Publication Data
Karlin, Bernie.
Night ride.
Summary: Riding in a car with his mother all night,
a young boy watches as the roadside landscape is transformed
from twilight all the way through to dawn.
[1. Night—Fiction] I. Karlin, Mati. II. Title.
PZ7. K14236Ni 1988 [E] 88-4436
ISBN 0-671-66733-5

NIGHT RIDE

To—
Our parents, Gertie & Harry, Mary & Morris
Our children, Lyle, Lee, Nancy, Sue and Peter
Our grandchildren, Matt & Ryan, Billy & Ben
And to all the other people who helped
make this book possible.

"Good-bye, Mom."
"Good-bye, Billy."
"Good-bye, Dixie."

"Good-bye, Dad."
"Good-bye, Susie."

We're on our way. Is your seat belt fastened?

PASSENGER CAR · $2.00

"Careful, Billy. Don't drop the money."
"I won't, Mom."

"Wow!"
"Pretty, isn't it, Billy?"

"It looks like it's going to crash, Mom."
"It's coming in for a landing."

"What happened?"

"Do you think we could go?"
"We'll talk to Daddy about it when we get home."

"Look, it's all lit up."
"They're playing a game tonight."

"Nighttime sure is busy, Mom."

"Phew! What's that funny smell?"

"A skunk!"

"It sure is spooky out here."

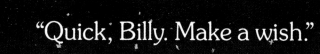
"Quick, Billy. Make a wish."

"Are you asleep, Billy?"

"It's going to be a beautiful day."